ALINA: *A Russian girl comes to Israel*

ALINA

A Russian girl comes to Israel

Story by
MIRA MEIR

Photographs by
YAEL ROZEN

Translated from the Hebrew by Zeva Shapiro

The Jewish Publication Society of America
5742 / 1982   Philadelphia

Copyright © 1982 by The Jewish Publication Society of America
First English edition   All rights reserved
This book was originally published in Hebrew by Sifriyat Poalim, Tel Aviv,
copyright © 1977
Manufactured in the United States of America

Designed by Adrianne Onderdonk Dudden

Library of Congress Cataloging in Publication Date
Meir, Mira, 1932–
Alina : a Russian girl comes to Israel.
Translation of: Alinah hi Ilanah.
Summary: a young girl who has recently come to Israel from Russia with her family
misses her old home and feels out of place in her new country. [1. Jews—Israel—Fiction. 2.
Israel—Fiction. 3. Emigration and immigration—Fiction] I. Rosen, Ya'el, ill. II. Title.
PZ7.M51585A   1982   [Fic]   82-15366
ISBN 0-8276-0208-1   AACR2

ALINA: *A Russian girl comes to Israel*

This is Alina.

She and her parents have just come to Israel from Russia. They now live in their new home in Jerusalem. Alina is in the third grade. There are many other children in her class, but she has no friends.

Her classmates think Alina is too proud to talk to them.

"She thinks she's so special," they say.

"Look at her, she keeps to herself, like some princess."

"She's stuck up. Just because she's new here she thinks she's great. So what if she just came from Russia!"

But Alina does want to make friends. She just feels uncomfortable in her new surroundings. There are so many new things here, things she doesn't understand and is too shy to ask about.

The games are unfamiliar to Alina. Even hide-and-seek, a game she played in Russia, is played differently in Israel.

When Alina first came to school she saw some children playing hide-and-seek and moved toward them. She was about to join the group when they did something she didn't understand. The children put their hands together and mumbled some strange words.

Alina tried to join them but they told her, "Not now, later."

Alina was upset and moved away. She assumed that no one noticed. "What's it to them," she thought, "if I play or not?" That's when her classmates began calling her "stuck up." They thought she was angry because she had been asked to wait.

Another day, at recess, the teacher saw Alina sitting alone and tried to help.

"Come on, Alina, why not join the others?"

They were playing a word game.

"Yuk," Gila muttered under her breath. "She hardly knows Hebrew. She'll spoil the game."

Alina heard her. "I'd rather not," she said.

"We were right, that Russian girl sure is stuck up," Michal told Gila.

Alina turned away. "Here in Israel I am a Russian," she thought. "In Russia I was a Jew."

The teacher was gone. She probably thought she had succeeded in getting Alina into the game and was no longer needed.

The teacher had once suggested to Alina that she change her name to Ilana, a Hebrew name, as if that would make any difference. If she did change her name that wouldn't make her any more Israeli. It was pretty foolish to think something like that could make a difference.

In class the teacher says that soon it will be Tu bi-Shevat. "What is Tu bi-Shevat anyway?" Alina wonders, but she is too shy to ask. Alina thinks about it all the way home.

Alina's street is brand new, with one building after another, all alike.

All of Jerusalem is built of stone. People say it's beautiful. "What's so beautiful about it?" Alina wonders. The stone is so harsh. She misses the Russian landscape she knew so well, the river that ran through the center of her town, the surrounding forests, and the friends with whom she shared so many secrets.

Alina comes to her house and is not eager to go upstairs. She knows her parents aren't home yet. Her father is at school. Her mother is working.

In Russia her parents were away most of the day too, but there Alina spent more time in school and when she came home her mother would be waiting for her.

Since there's nothing to do at home, Alina decides to take a walk.

Alina wanders out of her neighborhood to an area that is mostly rocks and dust. She feels as if the stone is pressing down on her, whispering. Again she remembers the green woods of Russia. Father was a forest engineer. He often worked far from home and sometimes, in the summer, the whole family would join him in the country. What wonderful berries grew there! And wild mushrooms! And there were always children to play with.

In Israel there are no real forests, only small wooded areas, no work for a forest engineer. So Father must go back to school to learn another trade. It's funny to see a grown man sitting and doing homework night after night. He sometimes even asks Alina's help with Hebrew words. She's so proud when she knows the answer!

But Alina's father is worried that he isn't working. It upsets him to be a student again. "It is only temporary," Mother tells him. "It will all work out. You'll see."

Father is silent.

"You'll soon finish your course. Then you'll be able to work," Mother assures him.

"It won't be the same," Father answers. "This is a new place and I'll have to start from the beginning. I'm not a young man any more!"

"But Boris," Mother says, "we are in our own country. We knew it might be hard at first, but we are among our own people now."

"That's right," Father says. But Alina knows he is not convinced.

Alina walks on. She hasn't eaten anything since breakfast. Should she try some *falafel*? It smells so good. Everyone is so crazy about it!

Alina sees a *falafel* stand and watches the curly-haired *falafel* man roll balls of mashed chick peas and drop them, carefully, into the sizzling oil. Alina buys a *falafel* sandwich and bites into it.

"It's too spicy," she thinks. "How could anyone like this awful stuff?"

It's late. Time to go home.

Alina realizes how far she has wandered. She has some money left and decides to take the bus home.

The bus is crowded. Alina notices an Arab wearing a *kaffiyeh* on his head, and a tourist couple, probably Americans. At the next stop a bearded Jew with earlocks and a wide hat gets on. So many different kinds of people in one city!

Finally it's Alina's stop. She gets off and sees her mother standing in front of the house, looking up at the sky. What is she looking at?

"The sky is so blue, Alinotchka," her mother says. "Tell me, have you ever seen such a beautiful blue sky?"

"Everything here is beautiful to her," Alina thinks. "But not to me."

Alina goes to a special language class for immigrant children. The teacher, Rina, is nice, and Alina enjoys the class.

"Why such a long face, Alina?" Rina asks.

"What is wrong with my face?"

Rina laughs. "No, it's not actually long. That's just what we say here when someone looks gloomy. Understand?" And she bursts into laughter again.

"I have another question," Alina says. "What are the strange words they mumble here when they play hide-and-seek? And why didn't they want me to play with them? Why did they tell me, 'Not now, later?'"

"That's simple," Rina says. "Before they start playing they put their hands together and say *en-de-ah-tru-ah*. It's just a way of deciding who will be 'it.' This takes an odd number of players. When you came along they probably had an odd number already."

"That's right," Alina says. "There were five of them."

"So that's why they told you, 'later,'" Rina explains. "You would have been the sixth, and they couldn't start with an even number."

"Now I get it," Alina says. "But when it happened I was upset. I walked away and no one even noticed."

"It seemed that way to you," Rina says, "but I'm sure they did notice. In fact, they probably didn't understand why you left."

Alina's questions come popping all at once.

"One more thing, Rina. What is Tu bi-Shevat?"

"It's a holiday in honor of the trees," Rina explains.

"What do you mean?" Alina asks.

"Trees are very important in Israel. In fact, many girls are called Ilana, which means a young tree in Hebrew. On Tu bi-Shevat you will have a chance to plant trees with your class. It will be fun for you and your friends to watch the seedlings grow."

"It won't be fun for me," Alina says. "I don't play with Israeli kids. I'm afraid they'll laugh at me and make fun of my Hebrew. One of the girls invited me to her house but I didn't go."

"Listen to me," Rina says. "Israelis are not always polite. They tease a lot. They're known to be tough on the outside but soft on the inside, like the *sabra* fruit. If they invite you to their house I'm sure they want you to come. When you don't know a game or a word, ask, and someone will explain it to you. If you don't speak up, if you run away, they'll probably think you're strange. Now come here and let me see your homework."

Tu bi-Shevat arrives at last. In school everyone gets a small seedling in a tin can. Alina doesn't know what to do with it. In Russia she had seen huge oaks being cut down, but she had never done any planting.

'I'll show you what to do," Rutti offers. "I know, because we do this every year on Tu bi-Shevat. You set the plant in the hole, carefully, without loosening the soil that sticks to the roots. Cover the roots and make sure the soil is firm. Then you press down with your feet gently. Remember, the plant is very delicate."

The two girls work together.

During recess Rutti asks Alina, "Would you help me with my math? I don't understand these new problems."

Alina doesn't know what to do. She understands the math very well. She learned it in Russia the year before. She could explain it easily. But Hebrew is such a strange language, with such confusing rules. Rutti might tease her if she makes a mistake and says "third" instead of "three," or "ninth" instead of "nine."

"Well," Rutti says, "why don't you answer me?"

Alina remembers what Rina told her. She doesn't want Rutti to think she's unfriendly.

"OK," Alina says. "I'll explain the math to you if you help me with the Bible homework. How's that?"

"No problem," Rutti says. "Come to my house this afternoon. I live at 53 Ha-Hagana Street. Make it about 4. OK?"

Alina can hardly wait. At last she is going to an Israeli home. She hopes she will not feel as uncomfortable as she does in school.

Alina worries all the way to Rutti's house, but when she arrives she is immediately reassured. Rutti answers the door. Her mother brings them fresh orange juice and cookies.

The Bible homework is easy, even interesting. They read about King David and Absalom, his son. And Rutti catches on to the math very quickly.

"Let me fix your hair," Rutti says later. "Those braids look babyish. You're in third grade now! A ponytail would be much better." Rutti combs out Alina's hair and ties it in a ponytail. Alina looks in the mirror. The new hairdo makes quite a difference. She wonders how her mother will like it.

At home, Alina's mother is pleased with the new hair style, though it is a little hard for her to get used to it.

"By the way," Alina's mother says, "we're going to a kibbutz this weekend, to visit some cousins. It's a long trip. I hope it will be fun for you. They have a girl your age."

In school the next day the teacher says they will be talking about new immigrants. It is only then that Alina notices how many of her classmates are newcomers: Ronni from France, Tom from the United States, Shlomo from Iran, Hava from Argentina, Eliyahu from Russia, and, of course, Alina.

"There are Jews in many countries throughout the world who are eager to come to Israel," the teacher begins. "They often have a hard time getting permission to leave. Many of those who come have difficulty with the language, the climate, finding work—but they all want to be Israelis." Alina doesn't remember raising her hand, but she suddenly realizes she is talking excitedly.

She describes her own family, her father "the student," the new neighbors—a mother and two girls whose father is still in prison in Russia because of his Zionist activities. She tells about their baby named Geula, which means "redemption" in Hebrew. Geula has never seen her father, and the family hopes that he will soon be released from prison and allowed to join his family in Israel and share their *geula*!

Everyone is listening attentively.

"Is it really me talking on like this?" Alina asks herself in disbelief.

"Since there's no homework today," Rutti says to Alina after class, "let's go to the Old City. My mother will come with us."

This time the city looks much more attractive to Alina. The stone no longer seems harsh. The narrow alleys, sparkling domes, and smiling people are now beautiful to her.

"There's the Tower of David," Rutti says. "It really belonged to King David. We just read about it in our Bible homework. Remember? Should we stop and look at the Pillar of Absalom? Remember him? David's son, the one who rebelled because he wanted the kingdom for himself."

"Of course. Let's go," Alina says.

At the Western Wall they notice some men with fur hats, long black robes, beards, and earlocks. In Russia Alina had never seen such religious Jews. "Aren't they afraid to let anyone know they're religious?" Alina wonders. Then she remembers that things are different in Israel.

On the way home the girls pass the schoolyard. The new plants are drooping. "It's hard for them to take root," Rutti explains.

"I'm going to a kibbutz tomorrow, right after school. It's near the border," Alina tells Rutti.

"When will you be back?"

"After Shabbat," says Alina. "And on Sunday I'll be in school."

"Have a good time," Rutti says.

36

Alina is excited about going to the kibbutz. She pictures it in so many different ways.

When Alina arrives there with her family she is sure they are in the wrong place. Small white houses are scattered all around parklike grounds.

"If a kibbutz is a farm," Alina asks her cousin Hadas, "where are the cows, chickens, and horses?"

"Our animals are kept in one central area," her cousin tells her. "We share all the property. The cows are in a barn that's so spotless it looks like a clinic and the chickens are all in a big building that looks like a factory.

"I see lambs over there," says Alina. "Can I pet one? Can I pick one up?"

"Sure," Hadas answers. "Here, try the one with the brown ears."

"It's nice to hold something so soft and warm."

Suddenly a loud alarm sounds.

"Come quickly!" Hadas says. "There's an attack some-where in the area."

The girls run to the shelter where they find their parents as well as Hadas's entire class.

"We're used to the shelter by now," Hadas says. "It's like home to us. We sometimes stay here for days. Look around—we have everything we need. Food, games, bathrooms. We can live pretty well in here."

"It's awful," Alina thinks. She can't help feeling a little frightened. But everyone else is calm.

One of the men comes in from patrol. "There's nothing to worry about," he says. "The shells are falling quite some distance away. Still," he adds, "the army is asking us to remain in shelters for a while."

The children go back to their games.

Hadas invites Alina to play a word game. "But I don't know much Hebrew," says Alina timidly.

"That's all right," Hadas answers. "We'll help you."

Alina doesn't go back to Jerusalem when Shabbat is over, or even on Sunday. She spends two days in the shelter, then one more day in the kibbutz because travel is restricted on the roads near the border. It is Monday before she is able to go home.

"Alina is coming! Here comes Alina!" the children shout when they see her approaching the school yard.

"We were so worried about you," they say. "Were you really in a kibbutz near the Lebanese border?" Ronni asks.

"Rutti told us that's where you were going. We heard about the shelling on TV. What was it like?" Gila asks.

"I spent two days in the shelter," Alina tells them.

"Were you afraid?" Rutti asks.

"Yes," Alina admits. "But everyone else was calm. They're used to it."

Alina can't help wondering if they really were worried.

"I don't know what's come over Alina. She's changed so much," Gila whispers to Michal. "She's not stuck up anymore."

"Alina," Rutti says. "Did you see the seedlings we planted on Tu bi-Shevat? Yours is doing so well."

"You know something, Rutti," Alina says, "people are like plants. When they're small they can be moved easily from one place to another. At first it's hard for them to take root. But, after a while, once they begin to settle into the soil, it's almost impossible to uproot them."

Alina pauses for a moment. She seems lost in thought. Then she says, "I think I would like to be called Ilana, after all. It's a nice Israeli name and it suits me, doesn't it? Ilana means a young tree. Right? And it sounds like Alina, too."

A few days later a new girl comes to Ilana's class. Her name is Sonia. She has just arrived from Russia. Sonia doesn't know the language or the games in this new country. She keeps to herself.

"Come on," Ilana says to Sonia. "You can play with us. I'll show you how."